For

Phyllis Fogelman

First published 1996 in Great Britain by
Walker Books Ltd
87 Vauxhall Walk
London SE11 5HJ

First published 1995 by
Dial Books for Young Readers, New York

Text © 1996 Rosemary Wells
Illustrations © 1995 Rosemary Wells

This book has been typeset in Cochin.

Printed in Hong Kong

British Library Cataloguing in Publication Data
A catalogue record for this book is
available from the British Library.

ISBN 0-7445-4486-6

EDWARD'S
FIRST DAY AT SCHOOL

ROSEMARY WELLS

WALKER BOOKS
AND SUBSIDIARIES
LONDON • BOSTON • SYDNEY

Monday was the first day of playschool.
"Are you ready, Edward?" asked
Edward's dad.

But Edward was not ready.
So his dad helped him to get dressed.

Edward's mum fed him
his porridge.

Together they put him
into the car.

But Edward got out again
to get Bunny.

I'll hide, he thought, and
they'll never find me.

But they did.

Back went Edward into the car.
His seat belt was securely fastened.

"Now we are ready at last!"
said Edward's mum.

At school Edward's teacher
was all smiles.

Everyone was happy and busy.

But Edward didn't want to be
happy and busy.

Edward wanted to go home.

On Tuesday, Edward didn't want
to paint.

On Wednesday, he didn't want
to slide.

On Thursday, he went into the
wrong washroom.

"OH, NO!" said the girls.

On Friday, Edward's teacher said,
"Not everyone is ready for the same
things at the same time."

"Well, we'll just take him home
until he *is* ready," said Edward's
mum and dad.

"Be ready soon!" shouted
everybody.
"I'm ready right now," said Edward.

"What are you ready for?" asked
Edward's dad.
"I'm ready for my sandwich," said Edward.

"And Bunny is ready for
his bug soup!"